IT'S PERFECT BEING ME

Robert O. Martichenko

Illustrations by Blueberry Illustrations

It's Perfect Being Me
By Robert O. Martichenko

ISBN: 978-0-9970308-6-0

Blueberry Illustrations is a world class illustrations and self publishing company for children's books and other books. The illustrators of Blueberry Illustrations are recipients of various awards and nominations. More than 350 books have been illustrated and published by the company and many more are in the process.
www.blueberryillustrations.com

DEDICATION

To all people, children and adults,
May you embrace and enjoy the *Perfect You*.

Retreat

One, two, three,
Is really pretty easy.
ABC,
Isn't that tricky.
But when I try to go farther,
I find it starts to get harder,
So I retreat back to the simple things that I know.

I moved to a new school this year,
But fitting in was a challenge for me.
So many groups to choose from,
It was hard to decide whom to be.

I tried to be a comedian,
Humoring people as I spoke.
But I had to explain the punchlines,
When no one laughed at my jokes.

I tried to be a tough type,
Asking little kids to step aside.
But if I ran into a bully,
I'd run away and hide.

I tried to be a big strong athlete,
Excelling at every game.
Until I took a dodgeball to the head,
And walked away in pain.

I tried to be a super dude,
Standing around and acting cool.
I showed up at my first party,
And didn't break a single rule.

I tried to be a talented artist,
Creating beauty from thin air.
My inspiration for a painting,
Was a picture of my chair.

I tried to be a clever politician,
Performing a speech for my campaign.
But when my classmates went to vote,
They could not remember my name.

And I tried to be a hipster,
Ignoring the latest trends.
Then I came to school one day,
Dressed just like my friends.

I tried joining a rock band,
Playing guitar and singing songs.
But I don't carry a tune so well,
So I could never play along.

Then I tried the drama club,
Acting on stage with lights and sound.
The part I got had just one line,
Which I forgot when it came around.

I tried to be the star student,
One hundred percent on every test.
But after studying for my math class,
My brain needed a rest.

I tried being the teacher's pet,
Bringing an apple every day.
With every question I'd raise my hand,
But never knew what to say.

And I tried to be Miss Popular,
Good looking and clever as can be.
But my friends didn't get the message,
'Cause nobody noticed me.

Robert O. Martichenko is a Canadian-American entrepreneur, writer, poet, public speaker, and podcaster. On a perfect day, Robert can be found hiking in the mountains with his family, friends, and faithful yellow Labrador Retrievers. Robert is interested in making the world a better place by focusing on stories that promote kindness, respect, and empathy.

Robert is also an award-winning novelist.

Drift and Hum is a captivating novel about the kite ride of life and dealing with obstacles along the way. The story is told through the eyes of Sam, a 50-year-old South Carolina man who reflects from the present day back to his Canadian childhood to make sense of all the challenges and universal entropy he has faced. His journey includes an extraordinary bond and friendship with three other boys as the four "Beaver Brothers" embark on adventure after adventure in their quest for peace of mind in the Canadian North and the American South.

Learn more at www.driftandhum.com